BIG BLUE & POLLY

WRITTEN BY MIKE DYKSTRA

ILLUSTRATED BY TIM READ

THE K CREW™

Bo and Grandpa H were sharing stories one afternoon. "You know Bo, it was about 1974 when Big Blue and Polly met for the first time," said Grandpa H.

"Wow! That was a long time before I was born," replied Bo. "Would you tell me the story please?"

Grandpa paused for a few seconds and then began, "It all started when two good friends, Jon and Bill, got together to build a bigger plow..."

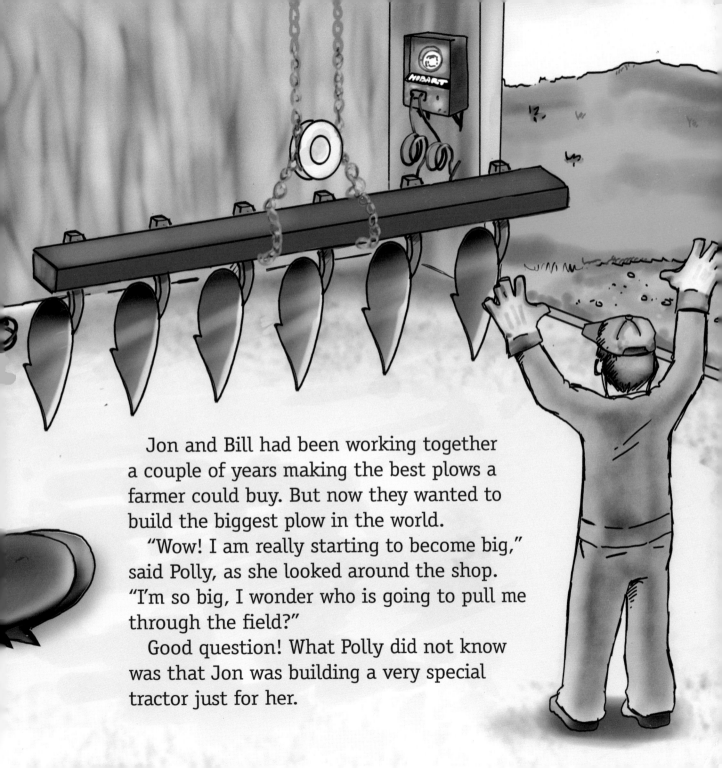

Jon and Bill had been working together a couple of years making the best plows a farmer could buy. But now they wanted to build the biggest plow in the world.

"Wow! I am really starting to become big," said Polly, as she looked around the shop. "I'm so big, I wonder who is going to pull me through the field?"

Good question! What Polly did not know was that Jon was building a very special tractor just for her.

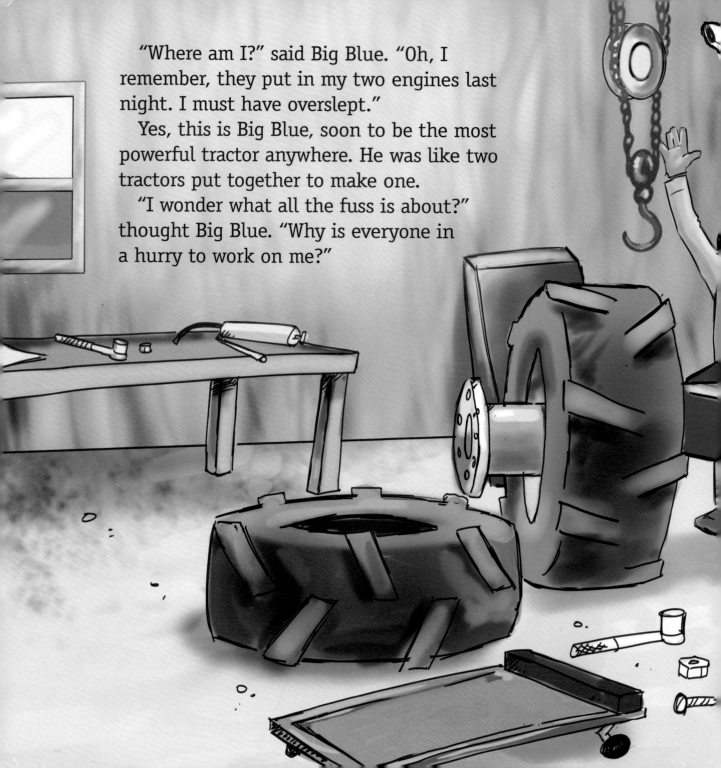

"Where am I?" said Big Blue. "Oh, I remember, they put in my two engines last night. I must have overslept."

Yes, this is Big Blue, soon to be the most powerful tractor anywhere. He was like two tractors put together to make one.

"I wonder what all the fuss is about?" thought Big Blue. "Why is everyone in a hurry to work on me?"

The next morning both Polly and Big Blue were brought outside. Jon was going to take them to the field later that day.

Big Blue smiled and said, "Hi, my name is Big Blue. What is your name? Do you have any idea why everyone is in such a hurry?"

"I'm Polly," she replied, "I heard Jon say we are going to a plowing contest in just four days!"

FOUR DAYS! They had to be all ready to plow together in just four days! Big Blue and Polly were not sure it could be done. But Jon and the other mechanics worked day and night. They cut out metal parts, welded them together and put on paint.

Finally, the night before the plowing contest, Big Blue's shiny hood and exhaust pipes were put on. THEY WERE FINISHED! Tomorrow they will be going to the contest.

The two friends arrived at the show just in time. There were tents and people everywhere! Machines of all different colors were being washed and shined to look their best.

"Wow! This is a lot bigger than our shop," exclaimed Polly. "I hope we don't look silly in front of all these people!"

Finally, it was time to plow. Jon climbed into the driver's seat and Bill wished them all good luck.

"I don't think I can do this!" said Big Blue with a trembling voice. "There are so many people. I don't want to fail!"

"We would not be here if Jon and the others thought we could not do it," Polly responded. "We will plow better than anyone has before. NOW, LET'S SHOW THE WORLD HOW IT'S DONE!"

Suddenly, Big Blue's twin engines roared to life and he took off across the field with Polly kicking up clouds of dust right behind her! The crowds cheered! The other tractors and plows were quickly left coughing in the dust.

"I have never seen anyone plow so much so fast," a spectator shouted. The two friends just looked at each other and smiled.

"Let's really have some fun," shouted Big Blue, "let's dig in and show these folks what we can do!"

Big Blue first dug down in the dirt with his front wheels. Then he dug down with his back wheels. It looked like he was stuck.

"Hold on Polly!" he shouted, "we are going to take off!"

Big Blue revved his engines and then out of the ruts he jumped! Across the field they raced, never looking back!

"And that is how Big Blue and Polly showed the world how to plow. And since that day, they have been best friends," concluded Grandpa H.

"Thank you for telling me their story," replied Bo. "It is always good to remember that if we work hard together and encourage each other, we can do great things!"

COME JOIN US AT THE KINZE INNOVATION CENTER!

Visit us at the Kinze Innovation Center and we will show you the tractors, plows, grain carts, planters, and big other machines that tell the story of Kinze innovation! You will get to watch *The Kinze History of Innovation* in the movie theater and build grain carts and planters on touch-screen displays. You will also get to see some of the latest cool machines that Kinze is working on. So grab an adult and some friends and come see all of us soon!

ADMISSION IS FREE.

Open Monday – Friday, 9:00am – 4:00pm. Closed Saturday, Sunday & Holidays. Visit kinze.com for additional details and factory tour scheduling information (must be 14 years and older to tour factory).